Dedicated with love to my daughter Angela and my son Michael.

Angels

by
Patricia Richardson Mattozzi

Published by The C.R. Gibson Company, Norwalk, CT 06856

The C.R. Gibson Company
Norwalk, CT 06856

GB382   ISBN 0-8378-1843-5

Although I cannot see them,

I know that they are there,

for God has promised angels
to be with me everywhere.

When I rest, when I stand,
when I swing and slide,

angels all about me to comfort,
shield and guide.

And when I venture forth to do
something on my own,

how wonderful to know
that I am not alone.

When I run,

when I swim,

when I laugh and play,

angels share my every move
— throughout my busy day. —

Through the night a watch they keep,
while I rest and dream and sleep.

And when the sun peeks in my room,
and I rise to dress and play,

I thank you God for angels
that you have sent my way.

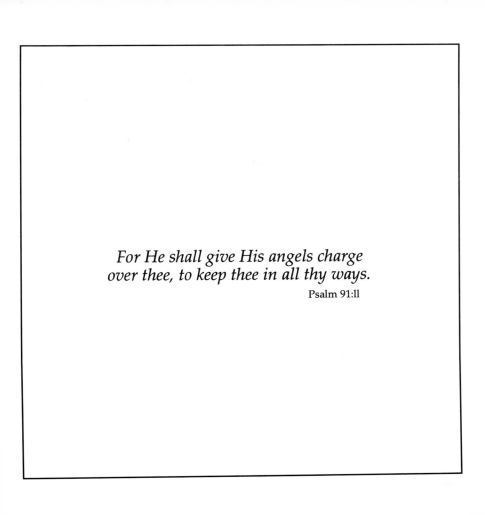

*For He shall give His angels charge
over thee, to keep thee in all thy ways.*

Psalm 91:11